For Amy and Joe
D. M.

To Scott and Joan for all their work
V. G.

First edition 2006

Library of Congress Cataloging-in-Publication Data
Martin, David, date.
All for pie, pie for all / David Martin ; illustrated by Valeri Gorbachev. —1st ed.
p. cm.
Summary: Grandma Cat bakes an apple pie that is heartily enjoyed by her family as well as the Mouse and Ant families that live nearby.
ISBN 0-7636-2393-8
[1. Cats—Fiction. 2. Mice—Fiction. 3. Ants—Fiction 4. Pies—Fiction.]
I. Gorbachev, Valeri, ill. II. Title.
PZ7.M356817All 2006
[E]—dc22 2005046917

2 4 6 8 10 9 7 5 3 1

Printed in Singapore

This book was typeset in Chesterfield D.
The illustrations were done in
ink and watercolor.

Candlewick Press
2067 Massachusetts Avenue
Cambridge, Massachusetts 02140

visit us at www.candlewick.com

All for Pie, Pie for All

David Martin illustrated by Valeri Gorbachev

CANDLEWICK PRESS
CAMBRIDGE, MASSACHUSETTS

Grandma Cat made an apple pie.

Little Brother Cat ate a piece.
Big Sister Cat ate a piece.
Momma Cat ate a piece.
Poppa Cat ate a piece.
Grandma Cat ate a piece.

One piece of pie was left.

And then the cats took naps.

“I smell apple pie,” said Grandma Mouse.

Little Brother Mouse ate a piece.
Big Sister Mouse ate a piece.
Momma Mouse ate a piece.
Poppa Mouse ate a piece.

Grandma Mouse ate a piece.
Six crumbs were left.

And then the mice took naps.

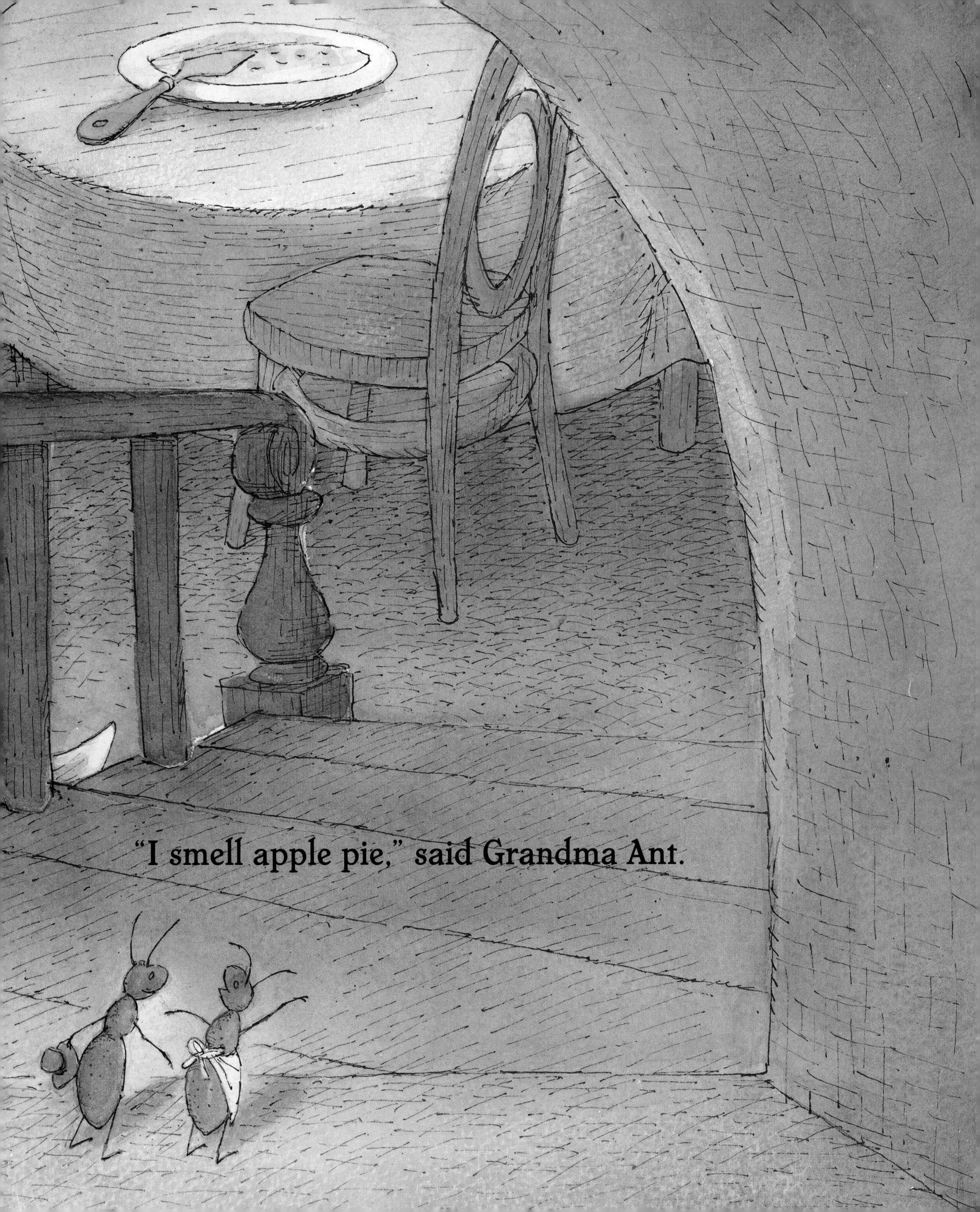

"I smell apple pie," said Grandma Ant.

Little Brother Ant walked away with a crumb.
Big Sister Ant walked away with a crumb.
Momma Ant walked away with a crumb.
Poppa Ant walked away with a crumb.
Grandma Ant walked away with a crumb.

One little crumb was left.

Then Baby Ant woke up from her nap.

"Pie!" said Baby Ant.

Baby Ant walked away with the last crumb.
Then the pie was all gone.

"I'm hungry. Should I bake another pie?" asked Grandma Cat.

"**Yes.**
Yes.
Yes.
Yes," meowed the cats.

"Yes. Yes. Yes. Yes. Yes," squeaked the mice.

"Yes. Yes. Yes. Yes. Yes. Yes,"

yelled the ants as loud as they could.

So Grandma Cat baked another pie.
This one was blueberry, and Brother Cat and Sister Cat and Brother Mouse and Sister Mouse and Brother Ant and Sister Ant and even little Baby Ant all helped make it.

SUGAR

And then everyone helped eat it,
until not even a crumb was left.